KU-428-987

ELMER AND THE WIND

David McKee

In Memory of Barbara —
with love and thanks for Chantel, Chuck and Brett

Andersen Press • London

It was a very, very windy day. Elmer, the patchwork elephant, was sheltering in a cave with his elephant friends, some birds and Cousin Wilbur, who was playing tricks with his voice. The elephants laughed when Wilbur made his voice come from a hole at the back of the cave.

"It's not a good day for flying," said a bird.

"It's a good day to be a heavy elephant," chuckled Elmer. "An elephant can't be blown away."

"I bet even you are afraid to go out in this wind, Elmer," said the bird.

"Afraid?" said Elmer. "Watch this then. Come on, Wilbur."

"Come back, don't be silly," called the elephants.

But Elmer and Wilbur had already gone out into the wind.

Once they were behind some trees and out of sight of
the others, Elmer led the way into another cave.
"You're up to something, Elmer," said Wilbur.
"Yes," laughed Elmer. "Make your voice come from

out there as if we were still walking away. Sound
like me sometimes."

"I get it," said Wilbur. His voice came from the
distance, sounding like Elmer, "It's hard to move in this
wind." Then like himself, "Careful, Elmer, hold on."

The elephants heard the voices and started to worry.
Wilbur called, "Hold on to something, Elmer. Look out!"

"HELP!" came Elmer's voice. "HELP! I'm flying."
Wilbur called, "ELMER! COME BACK! ELMER!
OH, HELP! HELP!"

"Elmer's being blown away, we must help,"
said an elephant.
    "If you go out you'll be blown away too,"
said a bird.
    "Form a chain, trunks holding tails,"
said another elephant.
    They crept out of the cave, each elephant holding
the tail of the elephant in front.

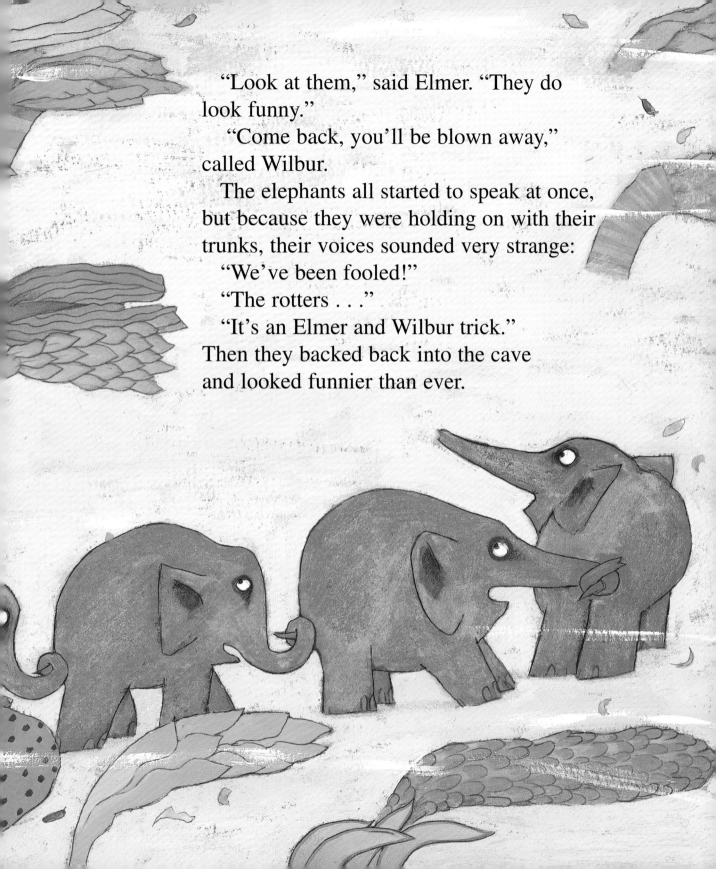

"Look at them," said Elmer. "They do look funny."

"Come back, you'll be blown away," called Wilbur.

The elephants all started to speak at once, but because they were holding on with their trunks, their voices sounded very strange:

"We've been fooled!"

"The rotters . . ."

"It's an Elmer and Wilbur trick." Then they backed back into the cave and looked funnier than ever.

When they were safely back in the cave, Elmer and
Wilbur returned as well. The elephants enjoyed the joke
but a bird said, "That was very silly, Elmer."

"But really, Bird," said Elmer, "an elephant can't be
blown away. I'll walk to those trees and back to prove it."

"Another trick," said an elephant, as Elmer walked away.

They watched as Elmer disappeared behind
some trees.

Then they heard Elmer's voice calling, "Help!
I can't keep on the ground."

The elephants laughed, "Very funny, Wilbur."

The voice came again, "HELP! I'M FLYING!"

The elephants laughed louder than ever.

"It's not me this time," said Wilbur.

"Look!" said a bird. "It isn't Wilbur."
The elephants stared; there was Elmer above the trees.
"What's he doing up there?" gasped an elephant.
"It's called flying," said a bird.
"Poor Elmer," said an elephant.

"It's my ears," thought Elmer. "They're acting as wings."
Wilbur and the others seemed very small as he flew away.

"This is really quite fun," thought Elmer after a while. He could see the other animals sheltering from the wind. They stared to see an elephant fly by.

"It's Elmer," said a lion. "I expect he's up to another of his tricks."

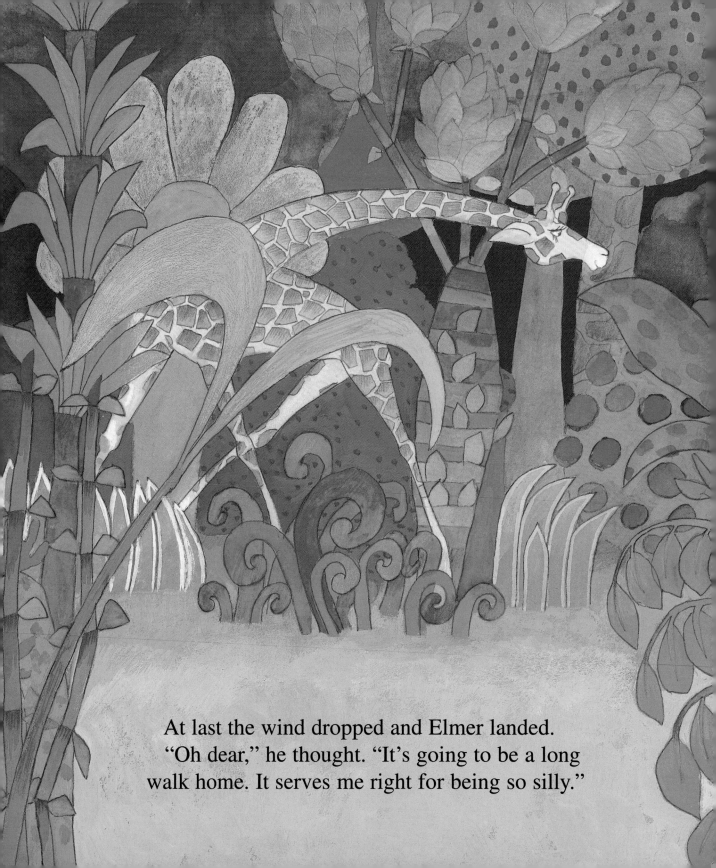

At last the wind dropped and Elmer landed.
"Oh dear," he thought. "It's going to be a long
walk home. It serves me right for being so silly."

When the wind stopped, the birds flew off to find Elmer and help guide him home. When at last the elephants saw the birds flying above the trees, they knew that Elmer was near. They rushed to meet him to hear about his adventure.

"You were wrong, Elmer," said the bird.
"An elephant can be blown away."
    "You were wrong, too, Bird," laughed Elmer.
"It was a lovely day for flying!"

DUDLEY PUBLIC LIBRARIES
L   47 4 37
667744   SCH
JY MAC

Copyright © 1997 by David McKee
The rights of David McKee to be identified as the author and illustrator of this work
have been asserted by him in accordance with the Copyright, Designs and Patents Act, 1988.
First published in Great Britain in 1997 by Andersen Press Ltd., 20 Vauxhall Bridge Road, London SW1V 2SA.
Published in Australia by Random House Australia Pty., 20 Alfred Street, Milsons Point, Sydney, NSW 2061.
All rights reserved. Colour separated in Switzerland by Photolitho AG, Zürich.
Printed and bound in Italy by Grafiche AZ, Verona.

10   9   8   7   6   5   4

British Library Cataloguing in Publication Data available.
ISBN 0 86264 595 6

This book has been printed on acid-free paper